Lions Club and our environment

Lions Clubs of the British Isles are doing our part to keep our planet clean, safe and healthy for future generations. We are pleased to share this storybook so you can learn more about how to help animals, plants, and sea creatures. We hope you enjoy reading about ways we can all look after the local places where you live, play and go to school.

This book belongs to:

.... *GAYWOOD LIBRARY* ....

....

This book has been kindly donated by:

.... *Kings Lynn Lions Club* ....

....

To find out more about how your local Lions Club gets involved in helping others, please visit www.lionsclubs.co

Thank you for helping Duffy, Marli and Nelson by looking after our environment!

For my children who never fail to show love and enthusiasm for nature - thank you! EJ

For my Dad, who passed on his love of art.
I hope this book encourages and inspires children to keep our seas and beaches clean. LC

First published by Under Pressure Media Ltd
Looe Cornwall PL13 1HT

Text copyright © Eleanor Jackson 2017
Illustrations copyright © Laura Callwood 2017

Printed sustainably in the UK by www.exwhyzed.co.uk   FSC

10 9 8 7 6 5 4 3

A CIP catalogue record for this book is available from the British Library.

ISBN 978-1-9997485-1-7

To find out more about Marli and the other Wild Tribe Heroes, plus teaching resources and how you can help, visit www.wildtribeheroes.com or Facebook, Instagram and Twitter @wildtribeheroes.

Marli's Tangled Tale

Story by Ellie Jackson
Illustrations by Laura Callwood

Under Pressure Media Ltd - United Kingdom

Out on the cliffs of a cool and green land lived a beautiful little puffin called Marli. She had come back from the ocean to the burrow where she had been born to lay her first smooth white egg which lay tucked safe and warm under her tummy.

Marli and her mate Rocky took it in turns to hunt for fish whilst tending their egg and they would slowly waddle out of their burrow onto the cliff edge then dive gracefully down the steep drop to the ocean below. Marli loved the freedom of gliding close to the waves before quickly diving under the clear blue waters to catch little silvery fish in her beak.

Inland and far away from Marli's home, the townspeople were excitedly getting ready for the grand opening of their new big store. The mayor was coming to cut the ribbon, there would be cakes and ice cream as well as a juggler, animals to pet and prizes to be won.

Hundreds of colourful balloons were going to be released into the sky, each one with a special number and a poem attached which read:

"Our new store is the biggest and the best. Can you tell us where our balloon came to rest?"

The children wondered if the balloons would travel as far as the farm or the woods or the river or even the sea! They all hoped that someone would find their balloon when it came down as then they would win the prize!

Finally the time came for the mayor to cut the ribbon and release the balloons! What a wonderful sight they made as they soared upwards, bobbing together one moment then floating apart the next. Sometimes a red balloon went highest and then next it was a yellow one!

The crowds clapped and cheered as the balloons went higher and higher until gradually they started to spread out and head for the countryside beyond the town where darker rain clouds had started to gather. The people packed up and went home, full of the joy and fun of the day, yet some of the children were starting to worry about what was going to happen to the balloons as they raced along towards the storm.

Soon the balloons had left the crowds and the town far behind and were floating over the distant patchwork of farms and fields in the open countryside. They were hurtling headlong into the storm clouds which were rapidly building on the hot summer's day.

The wind blew stronger, buffeting and hurrying the balloons along, whilst fat raindrops spattered angrily onto the balloons pushing them down in the cold air.

One by one the coloured balloons started to fall and some of their long silvery ribbons became tangled together.

Some fell from the sky onto the farms, some fell into the woods, some fell into the rivers and the last and biggest balloons fell far away onto the cliffs and into the sea. Down they all went to the ground they had started from, becoming trapped and tangled in the hedgerows and tree branches or ending up floating in the streams and rivers out to sea.

No longer were they bright and round with streaming ribbons, full of joy and summer fun. Instead they had become small wrinkled and shrivelled little things which were twisted and knotted, some had even burst and the happy little poems lay bedraggled and forlorn with no hope of being found by the people.

Marli's puffin colony had felt the storm gathering many hours before, and had called the alarm to each other. All along the cliff tops the little puffins had disappeared, sheltering from the wind and the rain in their dark and cosy burrows, keeping their precious eggs warm and dry.

Gradually Marli felt the raindrops which were pounding on the earth above her head start to slow and then it was her turn to waddle along the tunnel to start her hunt for fish.

Rain had made the cliff slippery and dangerous and waves were crashing onto the rocks below. Marli knew she would have to stick close to shore in case she grew tired battling into the strong winds.

She loved to skim the tops of the waves, flying close so she could see any fish below the surface, but when the waves were rough she knew she had to fly higher. She made several turns, her wings beating hard to fight against the wind when suddenly she saw a familiar flash of silver and she banked and swooped down, gliding effortlessly under the waves to catch at the fish.

Snap! Snap! Snap! went her beak and she eagerly waited for the wriggling fish to lie still but they danced and tugged at her, pulling her this way and that. Marli was confused as to what was happening, one of her wings felt tight and wouldn't flap. When she tried to call for help, her beak wouldn't open. She floated on the surface, paddling her legs furiously to try to get to shore but wave after wave pushed her around.

Time passed for Marli, day turning to night and night turning to day before the the wind died down. The sea became calm again with the sun brightening and warming Marli's cold body.

Her once graceful diving and swimming had become a desperate fight to reach the beach, but no matter how much she tried she kept swimming in circles, round and round until she was quite dizzy.

Weakened now and getting colder, Marli drifted onto the beach where she ended up amongst the seaweed and the plastic rubbish that had washed down from the rivers and been churned up by the storm.

Marli lay dreaming of her cliff top home and her smooth white egg when suddenly she heard voices calling to one another. She saw many people who had come to clean the beach of the plastic rubbish which surrounded her. Finally they found her, tangled in a silvery ribbon and trailing three withered balloons. The ribbon had wound itself round and round her, forcing her beak closed and trapping her wing to her side.

Gentle hands held Marli tight whilst the silvery ribbon she had mistaken for fish was cut free. Her wing was free! Her beak was free! But still the hands held her strong and safe. The people had seen birds like her before, weak and hungry and they knew she needed the help of the Wildlife Sanctuary before they could release her.

At the Wildlife Sanctuary Marli saw lots of other boxes filled with all different types of animals; seagulls, seals, foxes, rabbits and owls and luckily all of them had been found and rescued. Some of them had swallowed the balloons thinking they were food, others had become trapped in the ribbons like Marli.

One seal who had eaten a balloon would need an operation by the vets to remove it. If the balloons were left in the animals tummies or stayed tangled round their bodies then the animals could die. The vets and helpers had a lot of work ahead of them to make sure all the animals were healthy again and ready to be released.

WILDLIFE SANCTUARY
KEEPING OUR ANIMALS SAFE SINCE 1995

Marli thought of her egg waiting for her as she ate the fresh fish she was given. Quickly she grew stronger and stronger and was soon ready to be released back to her home. The kind people took her back to the beach where she had been found. Marli was carried down near to the waves and she grew excited as she recognised the sounds and smells of home.

The box was finally still and the lid was opened. Marli lay quiet for a moment, then as quick as she could, she flew up, higher and higher to the top of her cliffs, searching for her burrow amongst all the others. Calling to Rocky she finally heard his answer, knowing that he would be with their egg, keeping it safe and warm, waiting for her to come home.

Marli flew down and landed, waddling as fast as she could through the tunnel to tumble into their burrow. She felt for her egg, desperate to feel the smooth round shell she knew so well but all she could feel were feathers - the soft, downy feathers of her brand new baby puffling!

Her heart felt full of love for this tiny little baby and as she and Rocky looked proudly on, Marli knew that she had had a lucky escape and that she was free! Free of the balloons and the ribbons the people had put into the sky. Free to teach her baby to dive and swim, to swoop and fly in their beautiful home.

Did you know..?

There are three different types of puffin and they were originally named after the "puffed" shape of their bodies. They are about as big as a rabbit and their big colourful beak can hold several fish at once - the record number of fish counted in one beak was 62!

They live out at sea during the Winter and only come back to the land in the Spring to have their babies which are called pufflings. They dig tunnels and burrows like rabbits - sometimes they even use old rabbit burrows to save them the effort of digging their own.

Each male puffin will stay with their female puffin their whole life and they go back to the same burrows every year. They lay one single egg which both parents take turns to keep warm. Once the pufflings are born, the parents both help to feed and raise it until it is old enough to fly.

Puffins can flap their wings up to **400** times a minute and reach speeds of 88km/h which is about the same speed as a lion can run! They are fantastic swimmers and can dive down to 60m under water searching for their favourite fish.

Puffins are at risk from natural predators such as other big seabirds or foxes, weasels or rats. Like all animals, they are also in danger from plastic pollution in the sea which they can eat or get tangled in like Marli did.

Be a **Wild Tribe Hero** and help **stop plastic** in our **oceans!**

- Say no to balloon releases - pick something else that is fun to do instead
- Use less plastic – stop using single use plastic such as drinking straws and plastic bags – bring your own bags to the shops and say no to plastic straws
- Stop buying bottled water – carry a reusable bottle
- Recycle your rubbish at home and at school
- Go plastic free for your school lunch box
- Pick up litter you see around you if safe to do so
- Report injured wildlife to a local charity or vets
- Tell other people about the problem with balloon releases and plastics in the oceans and help spread the word by making posters and writing letters to save wildlife like Marli

YOUR actions WILL make a difference!

WILD TRIBE HEROES

Please share this book and its important message with your family, friends and teachers

How you can help Marli and her friends!

One way you can help to protect our marine wildlife like Puffins is to pick up litter when you see it. This can be as simple as collecting litter you see on the beach or in the park as you are walking along or you can ask your school or club to organise a clean up event. There are some things you need to do before you pick up rubbish to keep yourself safe:

1. Always go with an adult

2. Never pick up anything that looks nasty or is dangerous

3. Wear protective gloves and bring a bag to put rubbish in

4. Watch out for and don't touch sharp items like glass, needles, metal

5. BE SAFE NEAR WATER – Always follow safety signs. Look out for big waves, tide coming in or quick sand/mudflats. Be careful on the beach and near rivers, lakes and canals

6. Keep an eye on the weather and wear appropriate clothing and sun protection

7. Take a picture and upload it to social media using the hashtags #wildtribeheroes, #2minutebeachclean and #minibeachclean

8. Put the rubbish in a bin or take it home to recycle/upcycle